THIS BOOK BELONGS TO

To Guy and Astrid:
the rascal and little princess

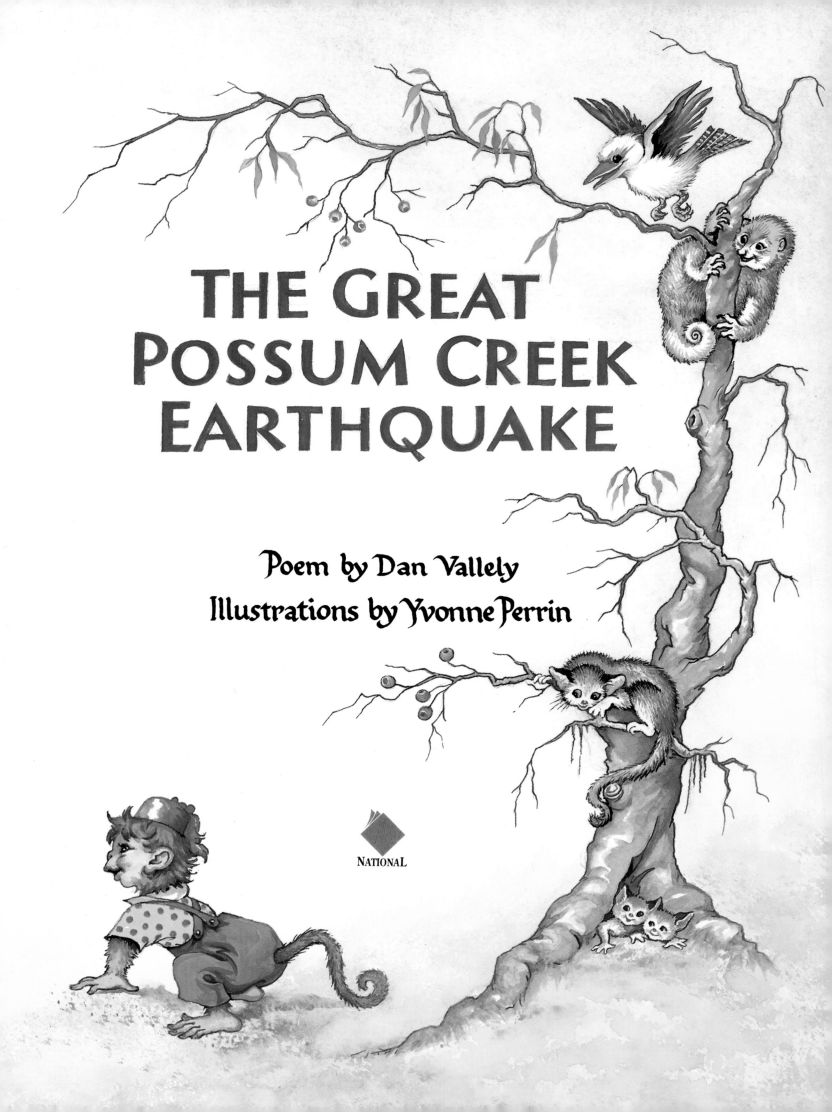

THE GREAT POSSUM CREEK EARTHQUAKE

Poem by Dan Vallely

Illustrations by Yvonne Perrin

NATIONAL

It was celebration week
In the town of Possum Creek
and a carnival was camped at Gecko Flats.
There were jugglers, funny clowns,
chimpanzees in fancy gowns,
fire-eaters and a troupe of acrobats.

GECKO FLATS

Platypus and Ed Galah
rode the cosmic rocket car,
Wally Wombat much preferred the carousel.
Old Professor Cockatoo
rode with Big Red Kangaroo
on the Spider, but it made him feel unwell.

They bought muffins freshly-made,
cups of icy lemonade,
and sat down beneath a shady ironbark.
As the friends enjoyed their food,
all around a multitude
had enormous fun throughout that
pleasant park.

They watched several ring events
and attended shows in tents,
They saw tigers and a lion named Lucille.
But no marvel could compare
with a ride up in the air
on the Super Dooper Giant Ferris Wheel.

They were at the very top
when it shuddered to a stop
and to their dismay the car began to shake.
The Professor said, ''Oh dear,
I'm afraid it's very clear,
we're about to have a rather strong earthquake!''

There was panic far below —
folks were dashing to and fro
and a car upon the Spider jolted free.
With two wallabies aboard,
like a cannonball it soared
and lodged high up in a eucalyptus tree.

Tents and sideshows all around
shook and tumbled to the ground;
just the Ferris Wheel defied that awesome force.
Then it parted from its base
and at very rapid pace
thundered off along a dried-up watercourse.

In its trim of green and gold
straight for Possum Creek it rolled
with our heroes hanging on for life and limb.
They were powerless indeed
as the Ferris gathered speed
and in truth their prospects looked extremely grim.

With astonishing good luck
not a single house was struck
as the speeding wheel continued on its way.
Peter Possum lost his grip,
bounced, and did a backward flip
through the window of the Drovers' Rest Cafe.

Through the piggery it sped,
as the frightened porkers fled.
Ed Galah fell off and landed with a thud.
Platypus was shaken loose
and he felt an awful goose
when he landed in the evil-smelling mud.

Then it cannoned off a rock
with a monumental shock
that ejected Wally Wombat from his seat.
Onward clanked the metal beast
on a path directly east
through a paddock filled with newly ripened wheat.

Then before a gaping crowd
into Wongi Lake it ploughed
ever deeper, and it disappeared from sight.
Although given up for dead,
the Professor and Big Red
both escaped unharmed to everyone's delight.

Though it hadn't been much fun
little damage had been done.
And despite their share of fearfulness and pain,
as our little story ends
the Professor and his friends
have in truth emerged triumphant once again!

Published by
National Book Distributors
19A Roger Street Brookvale NSW 2100
First published 1993
Reprinted 1993

Poem © Dan Vallely 1993
Illustrations © Yvonne Perrin 1993

Printed in Hong Kong by South China Printing Company Ltd
National Library of Australia Cataloguing-in-Publication data

ISBN 1 86302 278 3